RETROSEXUAL

A FRISKY BEAVER STORY

AINSLEY BOOTH

SADIE HALLER

WWW.FRISKYBEAVERS.COM

Stew:
I haven't been the most attentive husband lately.

Adrienne:
He's the chief of staff to a brand new prime minister. I
get it.
But…

Stew:
Yeah. That "but". That's the problem. I've got a lot on my
plate, but none of it is more important than my marriage.

FOOTNOTES:

- No hipsters or metrosexuals were harmed in the
  making of this book
- This story takes place at the beginning of Prime
  Minister (Frisky Beavers #1), but can be read as
  a standalone silver fox story

THE FRISKY BEAVERS SERIES

*Retrosexual is a prequel short story to this series of full length
BDSM novels; it stands alone*

Prime Minister

Dr. Bad Boy

Full Mountie

Mr. Hat Trick

Page of Swords

Bull of the Woods

Private Citizen

Visit www.friskybeavers.com to learn more!

1

STEW

"DON'T WORK TOO HARD," she says to me as she kisses me goodbye in the morning.

It's still dark.

We both know I'm not going to take her advice. So I kiss her instead, and I'm not quick about it. I love my wife. Not only because she packs my lunch every day, but because she pads to the front door with me—me in a suit that won't stay un-rumpled for more than an hour, her in a bathrobe I bought her three Christmases ago. And yes, I know a bathrobe is a terrible present for one's wife.

She's hard to shop for.

I'm also not talented in that regard.

But I can kiss her, so I do. A long, slow goodbye, my fingers tangled in her hair, my lips soft against hers.

I love the taste of Adrienne like this, all warm and undone. "Stay up for me tonight," I whisper against her mouth.

She stiffens. "You won't be home for dinner?"

So much for a nice kiss goodbye. I sigh and wince as she pulls away. "Did I say I would be? I can try."

"The kids haven't seen you in three days." She bites her lip and raises her eyebrows, expecting me to fill in the blanks.

I was traveling with the prime minister over the weekend, and we got home late last night. And I'm sneaking out at the crack of dawn because right now, my job is trumping my role as Dad.

But it's a big week.

We've got a slate of new interns starting today, handpicked from graduate programs across the country. They're going to work closely with leaders, including the newly elected prime minister, to ensure that all voices are represented at the table, including our country's youth.

And before they arrive, I've got the PM's daily briefing and a metric ton of other work to clear off my plate so I can spend most of the day orienting the intern assigned to the PMO in between all the usual fires I'll need to put out.

On the other hand, my kids haven't seen me for three days. And my wife is glaring at me. "Right. Okay, I'll be home for dinner."

She shakes her head. "Don't promise me that if you don't think…"

She's right. I swear under my breath. "I'm sorry. I don't know when I'll be home. But I hear you, and I'll do my best."

Compromise and honesty might not be sexy, but they've served us in good stead. We had no idea what was going to happen when the last government toppled and the election was called.

No idea that Gavin Strong Fever would sweep the nation, and my candidate—the thirty-nine-year-old bachelor from Vancouver, the fighter, the hockey player, the man of the people—would lead his embattled party into an unexpected victory.

Yes, I knew he had appeal. And smarts. And a huge amount of drive and commitment to his country.

Both personable and incredibly capable, Gavin is a smart, switched-on guy. But smart and switched-on don't always resonate with the voters.

I knew we'd represent well, and get the party a few more seats than the pathetic two we'd held before the election.

I had no idea we'd sweep to power.

Or that I'd end up the chief of staff to the nation's leader, and my wife would suddenly be solo-parenting our three kids.

It was supposed to be a whirlwind election. Now it's going to be a whirlwind four years in power. At least.

I tug her close. "I love you. I will do my best. And if you fall asleep before I get home tonight, I won't wake you up."

"You can wake me up," she whispers, brushing her mouth against mine. "We can be quick."

Deep inside, need roars to life. Even after all these years, this woman is everything to me. "One day…" We'll take our time. One day, we'll sleep naked and wake up late and have all the time in the world.

She laughs. "I know. One day."

But not this day. And probably not this night, either.

THE NEW INTERN is a PhD candidate from the University of Ottawa, Ellie Montague. She seems even smarter than promised by her CV. Unfortunately, by mid-morning I'm pretty sure she's regretting taking the three month position because it's what I call a *Gavin's Not Happy* day.

Don't get me wrong. My boss not being happy is a good

thing. It means he's zeroed in on a problem and he's going to fix it.

This is why we're in government. This is why I never see my wife and kids—because we're going to fix shit.

It just comes with a good dose of yelling when incompetence is uncovered.

Today's furor is over fundraising and lobbyists. It's a legitimate concern, one on which we want to distinguish ourselves in a big way from our predecessors, but we've got a private event in five weeks that could need to be chopped if the PM decides to take a hard line on influencers.

So after Gavin lays down the law—pivot the fundraiser or ditch it completely, because we will *not* be in the pockets of the wealthy—I pull Ellie into my office for a working lunch. Orientation is over, welcome to the real mess.

"Sorry about this." I gesture to the stacks of briefing books on my desk. "I suppose I should take you out to lunch for your first day, but this is the pace at which we work."

"It's fine," Ellie says, giving me a smile that quickly fades to a serious look. "What do you need me to do?"

There's something about this one. I think she means it, like she really wants to make a difference. Of course she's still got stars in her eyes about the PM—they all do, it's a fact of life. But she's doing her best to lock that down, and I respect that.

I pull out my lunch. Adrienne made ham and Swiss on rye, extra-tall, so I can spare half. "You want some?"

Ellie gives me a surprised look. "Sure."

"Feeding you is the least I can do."

She laughs. "Not literally."

"Okay, it's the least my wife would allow me to do." I point to Adrienne's picture on my desk. "She made the sandwich, so it's divided by her rules."

"That's sweet." She says it like she knows she's supposed to, but it really is. That's my wife. I'm a lucky man, but the bar is set high.

I dig two cans of Diet Coke from the box under my desk and hand her one. She cracks it open with one hand while she reaches for the file on the fundraiser.

We eat in silence. Five minutes of chewing and thinking, and for the last half-minute, Ellie's forehead pulls tighter with each quiet tick of the second hand on my clock.

I lean back in my chair. "What do you have?"

"One problem with him saying that over and over again is that he's rich, too," she points out, licking mustard off her fingers. "And everyone knows it. Don't get me wrong—most people like that about him. But he's hardly one of us with the sandwiches from home."

I snort. "Don't let him hear you say that."

"He's a man of the people in many other ways. He knows how much a loaf of bread costs, that's all that matters. But he's also comfortable with these donors, right? What if it wasn't a fundraiser for the party? What if it was…like a kick-off for a community challenge?"

"Keep talking." I root around in my lunch bag for the best part. "Chocolate chip cookie?"

She shakes her head. "But I'll take another pop if you've got one."

I toss her another Coke.

She takes a sip, then leans in. "He shouldn't shut himself off from business leaders. He needs to stay connected to them, and show them who's boss. Canadians just want to know that he's not in their pockets. They'll be thrilled if he can turn it around, make them bend to his will."

"Shit." I rock back in my chair and shove the rest of the cookie in my mouth. "That's good."

So good I want her to present it tomorrow at the briefing. She blanches, but agrees. I like that spirit, and I'm about to reassure her that it's really not as scary as it sounds when Gavin appears, bursting into my space without so much as a knock. "This report from the Ministry of the Environment is fucking bullshit, Stewart."

"I'm in a meeting, Gavin." I sigh and gesture to Ellie.

Gavin twists around, his attention now firmly on my guest. "Ms. Montague. Would you step outside?"

Jesus, this can't be good. And given that Ellie's somewhat of a guest in our office, and it's her first day…I open my mouth to protest, but she beats me to it, giving him a firm look. "I'd rather stay."

I almost laugh out loud at way Gavin freezes. He wasn't expecting that.

"Sir," she adds, flushing a little. "I'd rather stay, sir. Because…I'm the barometer, right? Without me, you're talking in an echo chamber. That's what you said in your announcement about these internships." She turns her attention back to me. "I don't think your office is an echo chamber, of course, Stew."

I grin as Gavin laughs. That cuts the tension, because no, I don't have any problem telling the PM when he's wrong, and he says as much to Ellie.

She lifts her chin. "Okay. So what part of the report is fucking bullshit?"

He laughs and turns back to me. "This one can stay."

"Glad you approve," I mutter, rolling my eyes. "Now can we get this meeting back on track? I'm already a few hours behind in my day and I promised my wife I'd be home before dark."

THE LAST THING I do before I leave the office is fire off

another email.

Checking for—and replying to—the response is the first thing I do when I pull into the driveway of my dark house. All the lights are off, and my heart sinks.

I knew it was late, but…

It's not always going to be like this. It wasn't like this when he was in opposition. There were late nights, but they weren't the majority of the time. And we didn't travel nearly as much.

I quietly let myself in. I'm hungry, but the first thing I do after dumping my briefcase on the bench in the entranceway and kicking off my shoes is head upstairs. The twins still sleep with their door open, so I stop in their doorway and look at them. They're both huge in their single beds…we need to move to a house with another room, but this place is close to Adrienne's school and a decent drive for me across the bridge, too.

I'm constantly thinking about you guys, even when I'm not here. That doesn't do anything for the worried guilt in my gut, though. And Daniel's door being firmly closed isn't good, either. I stop there and press my hand against the wood. *Especially you, son.* His younger brothers dominate Adrienne's time and energy. I backtrack downstairs and find a marker and a piece of paper. I scrawl **Daniel, Slayer of Dragons, or So Says His Father** on it.

Back upstairs, I tape that to his door.

Our bedroom is at the end of the hall. Our door isn't shut, but it's pulled to, and I wince as the door squeaks when I press it open.

I didn't need to worry about waking Adrienne, though.

She's in bed, reading.

She doesn't look up.

I'm sorry, I should say, but I know that's not enough.

"I'm going to Toronto next weekend. My sister's taking

the kids, so you don't need to worry about taking the time off work." She snaps her book closed. Still doesn't look at me.

"I tried to get home," I say quietly. "And something came up."

"Something always comes up. And tonight your kids were dicks to me. So I'm going away for the weekend without any of you." She turns off her light and rolls onto her side.

Fucking hell. I strip down to my boxer briefs and climb into bed behind her. When I touch her hip, she stiffens, but she doesn't pull away when I move closer, wrapping her smaller body in mine. We still fit perfectly together.

"It's not always going to be like this," I finally say out loud.

"I know."

"I love you."

She sighs. "I know that, you dolt. Just…it's hard on all of us. And today was a long day."

"My kids were dicks, eh?"

"Total dicks." She laughs. "And yes, on nights like tonight, they're all yours."

"And when they're hilarious and kind and smart, they're all yours." I kiss that tender spot behind her ear. "I'm not arguing with you. That's totally true."

"Rub my neck?" she asks hopefully. Like it's a big ask, and lately, maybe it has been.

"Always," I whisper, circling my thumb against her skin.

She falls asleep like that, with me stroking the tension out of her muscles. Before I can regret that we didn't do anything else, my phone vibrates from across the room.

It won't always be like this.

I just need to keep telling myself—and everyone else— that until it feels true.

2

ADRIENNE

THE FOLLOWING FRIDAY is a day off school for the kids, and my sister is happy to have them come early, so I take a vacation day to extend my weekend, as well.

I take the train from Ottawa to Toronto, and spring for a first-class seat. Four hours of wine and reading and no children or husbands annoying me.

Husbands.

Maybe that's the problem. I only have one husband. If I had two, it wouldn't be a big deal that Stew's job had become insane. I could have Work Stew, who I'm ridiculously proud of, and I could have... Home Stew. The guy who chops wood for our fireplace, who makes salsa from scratch—and then margaritas to match. The guy who likes to sleep in on Saturdays and go hiking on Sundays. Who puts the kids to bed and then comes to find me with a dirty grin that says it's my bedtime, too.

I miss that grin.

I miss his salsa, too.

If I could have a third husband, I'd pick Young Stew. I'm not sure he'd be interested in being married to a twenty-five-year-older version of his university girlfriend, but she'd be all over him and his youthful enthusiasm for late-night adventures and endless sex.

Although the real Stew has some advantages over his younger self. He's way more patient than he used to be. He knows my body better. He just doesn't get as many opportunities to prove his mastery of what makes me shiver.

I sigh and close my book. I really need this getaway, but I'm barely halfway to Toronto and I'm moping over how much I miss my husband.

But I'd miss him even more if I'd stayed home and he'd had to work.

He drove me to the train station. He had to leave work to do it. He came home and picked us all up. We dropped the kids at my sister's first, then he took me to the train station and helped me unload my bag. Then he wrapped me in his big, strong arms and kissed me.

He'd poured a lot into that kiss, and it left me breathless.

Now I touch my lips and think…okay. It's not always going to be like this. His mantra, and I believe him.

For now, I need to do some self-care. Adrienne Time, not Mom Time.

I twist around and find the first-class car attendant. "Could I have another glass of wine?" I ask, and she brings it right away. Ah, yes. Adrienne Time.

<hr>

I'M STAYING at a boutique hotel west of downtown. I don't have any specific plans, really, but once I check in, I open my suitcase and realize with a thud that I hate everything I've packed.

None of it says *night out in the city*. I'm not even talking about fancy shit. It's that none of it is *fun*. It's all mom clothes, and that's great for Ottawa. I'm a mom there.

I'm a mom now, too, but whatever. Whatever, indeed.

Okay, first step is shopping. I grab my purse and head downstairs.

The desk clerk calls out my name, and when I turn around, holds up an envelope. "This was dropped off for you, ma'am."

Shudder. I hate being called ma'am. I take the unaddressed white envelope with a polite thank-you. Inside is a piece of paper bearing the letterhead of a concert hall around the corner, wrapped around a general admission ticket for tonight. I don't recognize the band name.

I glance back at the desk clerk and hold out the ticket. "Have you heard of this band?"

She nods enthusiastically. "They're awesome. Should be a good show. There's a band from the nineties opening for them, too. Ever heard of The Replacements?"

I laugh. "Small world. They were my first real rock concert."

"Oh, how cool is that?"

Very cool. I look at the ticket. No note, but I have a sneaking suspicion who's responsible.

As I head into the sunshine, clear now in my goal to buy something to wear to a concert, I send Stew a quick text.

Adrienne: Thank you. You didn't need to do that.
Stew: Do what?
Adrienne: The ticket to see The Replacements.
Stew: That sounds like something I'd like to take credit for.
Adrienne: Huh. Someone left it for me at the hotel. Maybe it was meant for someone else…
Stew: Your sister?

Adrienne: I'll ask her. How's work going?
Stew: You know the answer to that. Are you having fun?
Adrienne: I'm going shopping.

I can practically hear his laughter from Ottawa.

Stew: I'm sorry.
Adrienne: I'm going out on the town tonight. I need to not look like a mom.
Stew: You're a hot mom.
Adrienne: Shut up.
Stew: I love you. Tight jeans and a tight t-shirt is always a good look on you.
Adrienne: Thank you. Get back to work.
Stew: Send me a picture.

I shake my head. Sigh. He's a good man, just a bit clueless. There's no way I'm wearing tight anything.

Except an hour later, after wandering in and out of a dozen shops, I find myself in a hole-in-the-wall t-shirt store just off Queen Street, and I fall in love with a v-neck tee with a wild skull painted on it. It's the kind of thing I'd totally have worn twenty years ago, and I want it now, if only for tonight, when nobody will know who I am.

"Can I try that on in a medium?" I ask the sales girl.

She rifles through the stack, then shakes her head. "We've got a small and a large. But they fit kind of generously, so I think the large will be too big on you. Try the small."

Nope. I haven't bought size small clothes since before kid number one was born. I shake my head. "It won't fit."

She just smiles and pushes it into my hands. "Give it a go."

I take the t-shirt, but I don't move. I glance at the other

designs on the table. "Which of these do you have in medium?"

She does a quick search up and down the stacks of fabric, with the kind of practiced eagle-eye hunting that only a retail pro has, and pulls out two options. I don't like either of them as much as the skull shirt, but I take the red one — because I don't want to come out of the change room feeling stupid because the small doesn't fit. Easier to pretend I liked the red one better.

Except once I'm in the change room, and I'm tugging the skull shirt over my boobs…it kind of does fit.

Only kind of. The v-neck helps. Man, when was the last time I showed this much cleavage?

The shirt is snug down my entire torso, but long enough to end at my hips. Lots of overlap over my jeans so nobody will see my mummy-tummy if I get excited and throw my hands in the air at the concert tonight.

I take a quick selfie and send it to Stew.

Adrienne: Tight enough?
Stew: Holy shit. Yeah. Love that.

Holy shit. A warm thrill wobbles through me. Okay, if he likes it. Maybe I can wear it as a sleep shirt when I get home.

I don't bother to try on the red t-shirt.

AFTER A DINNER AT A NOODLE SHOP — WHERE I read more of my book, uninterrupted, as I enjoyed hot food that didn't require any kind of compromise with family members or threats about being polite to eat it — I head back to the hotel to shower and change and get ready for my throwback to my youth.

The Replacements.

I think Stew first told me he loved me at that concert. He was drunk out of his mind, so I hadn't believed him, but then he said it again the next morning when I looked like something the cat had dragged in, so I believed him then. And I'd agreed to marry him a few months later.

I finish blowdrying my hair. Big, lots of hair spray. Then I do my makeup—more than usual, because my usual these days is lipgloss and mascara—and I send Stew another selfie.

This weekend was supposed to be just me-time, but I'm really liking this flirting from a distance thing, too.

Adrienne: Ready to head out and pretend I'm twenty again.
Stew: Damn, woman. Just remember you're mine.
Adrienne: I never forget that.
Stew: When a stranger hits on you tonight, the first thing you need to tell him is that your husband's a big guy who boxes with the prime minister.
Adrienne: LOL okay, baby
Stew: I'm serious
Adrienne: I love you so much
Stew: Good. Have fun.

There's a short line outside the concert hall, and I get in the queue behind a couple holding hands. I think of Stew, then I shake it off. Adrienne Time.

I need a beer.

The bouncer barely looks at my ID, then I'm inside. There's no line at the bar, so I pull a twenty out of my cross-body purse and order a bottle of Stella.

The crowd is a mix of ages. I'm definitely not the oldest person here, which makes me feel better. Lots of silver temples, just like Stew has, but nobody's in a suit. Lots of tight jeans—hello, hot guys—and visible tattoos.

I scoot down the bar, so I'm out of the bartender's way, but the show hasn't started yet, and I don't want to just randomly wander through the growing crowd when I don't have anyone to talk to. The bar makes a good base for people-watching.

Across the room, a thirty-something hipster guy catches my eye.

I smile and feel a hot blush spread across my cheeks. I'll have to tell Stew about that. He'll tease me mercilessly, but it'll turn him on a little to know his wife caught some young thing's attention.

The beer goes down smoothly, and since I don't have kids to worry about or a car to drive, I twist around and order another one.

When I turn back to the crowd, Hipster Guy is standing in front of me.

"Hey," he says.

He's taller than I thought from across the room. Almost as tall as Stew. Slimmer, with narrow hips and big feet.

Yes, I noticed his feet. And hands. I'm married, not dead.

"Can I buy you a drink?"

I lift my beer with a smile. "Just got one, but thank you."

"Are you here alone?"

I nod. "I am."

His gaze drops to where my left hand is wrapped around my beer. To my wedding rings. Oh God, I'm going to need to tell Stew how filthy this feels. When he drags his eyes back to my face, I'm still smiling.

He slowly steps past me and leans against the bar, waving at the bartender, who holds up his index finger. One minute. "I'm Fallon."

Is that even a real name? "Nice to meet you." I extend my hand. "Adrienne."

"And what do you do, Adrienne?"

"I'm a teacher." And a mom, a chauffeur, a wife, lunch-maker, peacekeeper…

"My sister's just finished teacher's college."

"Is she on the supply list yet?" I slip right into the professional stuff, and we talk about how hard the job market is until his beer arrives.

He holds his bottle up. "Nice to meet you, Adrienne."

I clink my bottle against his. "You as well."

"Maybe I'll see you after the show."

No, but it's a nice thought. "Maybe."

I watch him disappear into the crowd as activity starts on the stage. A roadie scurries across, setting a last guitar in place. Then the drummer comes out, the lights go down, and the crowd roars.

BY THE END of the second song, I've left the bar and pressed into the crowd myself. It's hot and sticky, and I'm grateful for the cold beer. I press the bottle against my neck, and the guy beside me takes a quick glance at my cleavage.

This is fun.

And the songs are totally taking me back.

I pull out my phone to text Stew, but I've got zero signal. Crap. There is a text message from him, though. I just can't respond to it.

Stew: Remember, I'm in Ottawa working.

What? That's…weird. Why would he think I'd forget?

I'm tempted to draft a reply, *remember, I'm wearing a tight t-shirt*, but with my luck, it wouldn't send until a random time much later and make zero sense.

Instead, I put my phone away. Okay, no more thinking about my husband in another city. Music and beer and fun.

From behind me, somebody bumps into me. Under the thump of the music, I hear a low apology, then a hand on my hip.

Whoa, hands off, buddy.

I spin around, and my breath catches in my throat. The hottest guy I've seen all night is standing in front of me. Dark jeans hug his thighs, and a black t-shirt with **you only live once** spelled across it hugs his broad chest and strains around his biceps. He's tall and big and giving me a totally obvious once over.

My skin warms under his appraisal.

He's holding a beer, and as I look up at him, he takes a long, slow sip. The way his mouth is a bit wet afterward makes my thighs tense up. The way his eyes are molten pools of heat makes the rest of me turn to goo.

I remember what I'm supposed to say. "My husband's a big guy who boxes with the prime minister."

He laughs and leans in so I can hear him. "Is that right? Why isn't he here tonight?"

"He's…in Ottawa working."

"His loss."

Oh, God. The heat radiating off his body slides under my skin and swirls around in my belly. "Really my loss," I whisper.

He leans in even closer. "I didn't catch that."

I hesitate, then push up on my toes and press my hand against his chest. "Never mind," I say, lifting my voice over the music.

3

STEW

GOD, she's radiant.

How long has it been since we've gone to a concert together? Since she's had a beer and listened to live music, my arms wrapped around her?

Not that we've gotten to that step yet. I'm still seducing her.

She likes this stranger, and my heart throbs a little at the reminder that we haven't shared anything like this in far too long.

It shouldn't have just occurred to me yesterday to do this. I should have more planned, but this was it. This was my entire plan. Fly down after work and find her at the concert.

Watching her get hit on was an unexpected bonus. I love the way she blushes. How she has no idea how fucking beautiful she is.

I brush her thick, dark hair off her shoulder, letting my fingertips graze along the bare skin of her neck. "Do you like this band?" I ask, knowing the answer already. I want to see her squirm.

"I do!" She hesitates. "Saw them a bunch of times when I was younger."

Every single time with me. "Yeah?"

She nods. "They're one of my favourites."

"Mine, too." I nod toward the stage. "I love this song."

She twists around, and I ease in beside her, my arm loosely around her waist, my hand on her hip. She doesn't move away from me.

What's going through her mind? How far will she let me play like this? I take a long slug of beer.

Against my hand, her hip shifts. Up, down. I glance at her as she starts to move to the music. She takes a drink, then shifts closer to me, her thigh rubbing against mine now. I hook my finger through her belt loop and step my far foot a bit wider, bracing myself in case anyone bumps into me — protecting her from the crowd.

That's how we watch the next two songs, her dancing on the spot beside me, wrapped in my arm at first, then she moves more in front of me. We finish our drinks, and the empty bottles get picked up by a passing employee. I put both hands on her waist now, rubbing the tight nip of her body, and lower onto the curve of her hips.

I throb for her. I'm ready to drag her back to the hotel now.

But I'm a stranger tonight. She wouldn't invite this man back to her room, would she?

I move my hands to her arms, then her shoulders. I duck my head and brush my lips against her ear. "Want another drink?"

She shakes her head. "I shouldn't."

"Do you have to call your husband to say goodnight?"

She shudders in my arms. It takes her a beat to jerkily shake her head. No. "Not tonight." She twists her head to the side, showing me her profile. "He's working late."

"Does he do that a lot?"

She nods.

"Dangerous, to ignore a beautiful wife."

She bites her lip. Oh, she wants to defend him. I rub my thumb along her jaw. "It's okay," I murmur in her ear as the song quiets. "I'll keep your secrets."

Her chest rises and falls, and like the other men here, I can't help myself but slide my gaze over her curves. But unlike those sad bastards, I know how soft and sweet the shadow between her breasts is. How her breath hitches when I circle her nipple with my fingertips, drawing her flesh into a tight, hard peak before tugging and twisting on it.

She gets so wet when I play with her nipples. Whiny and panting. She'll beg me for my cock if I get her worked up enough.

She finally twists towards me, her lips parted, her eyes wide. "I miss him," she whispers, and I almost miss it as the band amps up into the next song. "That's my secret."

I stroke my thumb back and forth as I nod. "Okay." I sway with her, almost dancing. "Well, you're not alone right now."

"No," she sighs.

I want to toss her over my shoulder and march her right out of here, but instead, I turn her back to the stage, and we watch the rest of the set, need humming hard in my bloodstream.

By the time The Replacements play their last song, we're both thirsty again. I guide her to the bar, my hand in the small of her back. I let it drift over the curve of her ass as we make our way through the press of the crowd, but I don't leave it there.

I don't want a stranger groping my wife's ass.

Not unless she wants him to.

We order two bottles of beer, then I turn toward her "Great shirt, by the way."

She tips her head back and laughs. "Thank you."

"Is that funny?"

"It's a long story."

"I've got all night." I ease her against my body, showing her how hard I am. How much I want her. How much I want to be what she needs tonight. "Are you staying nearby?"

She smiles knowingly, a brilliant transformation of her beautiful face. "Very tempting," she says, running her hand up and down my chest. "But I couldn't cheat on my husband."

I grin at her. "He'd never know."

"Oh, he'd know." She licked her lips. "Even when he's busy, he's observant. And I'd never be able to keep a secret like this from him. I tell him everything."

"No way."

She nods. "Yes way. I'll tell him about this."

"And what will he say?"

She takes a sip of beer and shrugs. "That you have good taste in women."

"He trusts you." It's a statement, not a question. I do, with my entire heart.

Another nod. "Of course he does."

"And you trust him, even with all those late nights at work?"

Her eyes crinkle. "Oh no you don't. Don't try to trick me into doubting him. You don't know my husband as well as I do."

Ha. That's probably true. Sometimes she sees me way better than I can see myself. "You figure?"

She takes a deep breath. "He's got a chance to do something huge right now. With the government. It's maybe a once-in-a-lifetime chance to literally change the world. It's all he can think about, and...I can't begrudge him that. I love him for that. Don't you get it? I love him because—"

I set my beer down and take her face in my hands. My amazing wife. I fucking don't deserve her. I lower my mouth to hers and pour everything into our first kiss of the night.

First, but definitely not the last. "Do you want to stay for the next band?" I ask her as she wiggles closer.

"Nope."

"Good."

As we tumble out the front doors, I almost run into two young girls. They're probably adults, just barely, because it's a nineteen-plus concert, but really...children. And I almost run into them because they're standing in the middle of the path joking about the "retro" band that opened for their favourite act.

I skid to a halt.

Adrienne gets between me and the children and whispers something at me, probably about not making a scene.

"The Replacements aren't retro," I protest.

"Does it matter?"

"They're wrong."

"This isn't like political ideology, baby. They're allowed to think what they want without getting a lecture."

"I don't lecture people about politics."

"I follow you on Twitter. Don't lie to me."

I haul her close and kiss her. "I want to go back to being the stranger seducing you into a one-night stand. He's not grumpy about politics or music."

"Ah," she whispers. "But I didn't want to have dirty sex with him in my hotel room. Only you."

"Dirty?"
"Filthy."
"Tell me more."

4

ADRIENNE

STEW HAS my jeans unbuttoned before we get into the hotel room. The short hallway is empty, but I'm still burning up with mortification as he strokes the bare skin of my belly above my panties. "Baby, I can't get the room key to work if you're undressing me."

He nuzzles the back of my neck. "Let me try it."

I spin around and press the card into his hand, then I return the grope, finding and cupping his erection through his jeans.

He can't get it to work, either.

"Fuck," he growls, and he cups the back of my neck, holding me still for a kiss before trying again. "Okay. Hands off for a second."

"That's what I said to you," I point out.

"You're irresistible. Not my fault."

My cheeks are going to hurt tomorrow from smiling so much. He finally gets the door open, and we stumble inside. He presses me back against the door—the private side, now—and runs his hands over the as-requested tight t-shirt. "This looks so good on you."

"Thank you."

"Now take it off." He helps, sort of, and pretty soon the t-shirt, my jeans, my heeled boots, and most of his clothes, too, are scattered around us.

"This is what that young kid wanted to do with you," he murmurs as he trails his fingers across my swollen, aching breasts. "He wanted to strip you down and touch you all over."

My husband is officially crazy. And adorable. I kiss the side of his jaw. "He was not seriously trying to pick me up. He was just being nice."

"I watched him. In his metrosexual shoes and his pretty-boy haircut. I watched him leer at my wife."

I laugh gently and pull him closer, happy for an excuse to run my hands over Stew's solid abs. "He was a hipster, not a metrosexual."

"How am I supposed to know the difference? Suddenly the music I listen to is retro. What the fuck?"

I laugh harder. "You're like the opposite of a metrosexual. You're a retrosexual."

He gives me a stern look that makes me shiver. "You're mocking me for being old."

"Noooo," I say in a bad attempt at solemn, inviting more stern looks. I duck under his arm and start to move across the room, tripping over his jeans.

"You're the same age as me."

"Not really." I giggle, and that pulls him up short.

His expression shifts from stern to confused. "How old are you?"

That sends me into peels of laughter. He growls as he chases me across the bed. "That was a serious question. I can't remember."

"I know, baby. I know. I'm two years younger than you."

He pins me to the bed, looming above me. "You look ten years younger."

I wiggle my wrist free so I can slide my palm over his very firm ass. "Not at all."

"Don't distract me with compliments about my butt. You called me old."

"Technically the teenagers at the concert called your music retro, which you interpreted as meaning old, and I just turned it into a thing. Hashtag retrosexual. Hashtag DILFs of Ottawa. Hashtag…"

"What's a dilf?"

"I'm really not telling you."

He wraps his hand around my upper arm. "I'll spank you."

"Promises, promises."

He rolls over and pulls me into his lap. He lazily swats at my bottom.

"Oh come on, put more into it than—ah!"

The sting of a proper spank always gets me wet. It also effectively ends all teasing, because he alternates each strike with a lazy, commanding stroke between my legs. After three swats, he pulls off my panties with rough efficiency, and continues to spank my bare flesh until I'm swollen and shamelessly grinding my mound against his thigh.

"What does dilf mean?" he asks again, his voice rough now.

"Dad I'd Like to Fuck. D-I-L-F," I spell out breathlessly.

His palm slows to a stop. "Do you have a list of them?"

"Just one name on it." I twist around and climb up so I'm kneeling, straddling his lap. "Stewart."

He groans as I trace a finger down his happy trail.

When I reach his boxer briefs, I slip my fingers into the waistband. He falls backward, bracing himself on his elbows, and I whisper for him to lift his hips before I slide the boxers part-way down his thighs.

Crawling back up his body, I pin his wrists to the bed, then lean down and kiss him. I rock my hips as I hover over him, my clit gliding over the tip of his erection, barely touching it.

He arches up, but not fast enough. I swallow his moans as I rise with him, never losing contact, but also never giving him the pressure he craves.

It's a heady feeling having the nation's most powerful DILF at my mercy.

But I want him inside me. Torturing him is torturing myself, and that wasn't on the menu for this weekend. I press down a little and slide up and down his cock for a few strokes, to sate my appetite, then I'm back to skimming it with my clit.

He grunts in protest, and as he pushes up again, I move with him, breaking the kiss as I do.

"You're only making this harder on yourself," I tease.

"I'm sure I'd have a witty comeback for you if my dick had left me any blood for brain-function."

"Don't worry," I say sweetly. "It's not your brain I need functional right now."

I nip his earlobe…his neck…his shoulder.

The tendons in his wrists flex as his hands clench into fists, and he moans as he makes a half-hearted attempt to break free.

I know he's bumping up against the limit of his self-control because I am, too. Yet he doesn't try to take charge.

This is my Stewart—putting my wants and needs ahead of his own when he can. Because more often than he'd like, he has to put the needs of the prime minster, and by extension, the country ahead of all else.

Taking pity on both of us, I ease all the way down on

him, increasing the pressure as I glide back and forth from root to tip.

I have the urge to work my way down his body and take him into my mouth, taste myself on him, and swallow him whole.

But I'm not that benevolent.

Not tonight.

Tonight, I want feel him deep inside my body.

I slide back up his cock, and this time I cant my hips until the tip of him is at my entrance.

I grin at him as I sink all the way down and grind my hips a little.

On the upstroke, I lean forward and kiss him, then pump my hips in short, fast thrusts over the head of his cock. When his fists clench and his wrists strain against my grasp, I plunge down, taking him as deep as I can.

I'm close and I want him to be inside me when I come.

As I bottom out, I grind my clit back and forth against him. Up, down, grind, grind. Stew pushes up against me, adding more delicious pressure exactly where I need it most. My control of the sex slips as he moves even more, driving into me now. We're both so close.

Then his hips jerk up and he pushes hard against me, the first pulses of his orgasm triggering my own.

And I'm lost.

Releasing his wrists, I collapse on his chest.

His heart beats fast and strong beneath my ear as he wraps me in his arms and kisses the top of my head.

I couldn't ask for a more perfect night. Or a more perfect husband.

5

STEW

I wake before dawn. Adrienne is curled up against me, her flesh warm and gloriously naked next to mine.

Not having any kids about to barge in is a good thing.

Being up at the ass-crack of the day is not.

I throw my forearm over my eyes, wishing it wasn't in my nature now to wake up so early. Then I hear my phone. Fucking hell. I hadn't just woken up as a matter of routine.

Cursing under my breath, I slide out of bed, tucking the blankets back around my wife to keep her warm as I dig for the offending device under a trail of discarded clothes.

When I find it, my stomach sinks. It's the prime minister. It's six in the morning here, but he's flown to his home riding in Vancouver for the weekend. It's only three there.

"You should be asleep," I say when I answer.

"Yeah. Can't. So I was thinking." Famous last words. "How do you feel about…"

I grind the heel of my hand into my eye socket and reach for the notepad and pen on the bedside table.

Slim, lovely fingers slide them into my grasp. I twist

around and see that Adrienne is up. She gives me a little shrug and a rueful smile. What can you do, her expression says. *I'll make coffee*, she mouths, pointing to the machine in the corner.

I turn my attention to the PM and the initiative he wants to task to two of his cabinet ministers.

By the time I've made the three follow-up calls necessitated by Gavin's idea, Adrienne is on her second cup. But she's still naked, so I'm calling this a win. "Have you had too much coffee to go back to sleep?" I ask as I rejoin her on the bed.

"Probably yes." She smiles at me. "How long do I have you for?"

"All weekend. I'm taking the train back with you tomorrow."

She doesn't look like she believes me.

I wince as I point to the phone. "No promises that won't ring repeatedly, but I don't need to be back in Ottawa."

Still not convinced.

Fair enough. I hook my hand around the back of her calf, right below her knee, and tug. "How about we just see how the day goes? I'm not busy right this second, for example." I press her leg out to the side and slide my palm up her thigh. "And I'm starving."

AFTER I GO down on Adrienne, we stumble into the shower, and she returns the treat.

Then we put on clothes and go outside. Adrienne insists on it, foolish girl. I'm pretty sure romance can be completely recaptured in bed, but this is her weekend in the big city.

She has an entire day planned, and despite my base

desires to take advantage of our kid and work-free time, I also want her to do exactly what she wanted to do before I showed up.

We start with breakfast at a cafe a few blocks away. It looks like exactly the type of place where Adrienne's admirer from the night before would hang out, and I tell her that as we peruse the menu.

The waitress swings by quickly with coffee then returns to tell us the specials. She gives us a few minutes, then returns once we've stacked our menus at the edge of the table.

"You guys know what you want?" she asks with a warm smile.

I order eggs Benedict and Adrienne gets the frittata of the day.

"Are you visiting for the weekend?" the waitress asks as she scribbles our order on her notepad.

"Something like that," Adrienne says.

I grin at her.

The waitress twirls her pen at me. "You're…oh, God, this is embarrassing. Like, I recognize you, but I've forgotten your name. But you work for the prime minister, right?"

Surprised, I lean back in my chair. "That's right."

She blushes. "I follow you on Twitter."

"Right. Cool." I'm not sure what else to say. This is the first time I've been recognized outside of a political convention or the immediate six blocks around Parliament Hill. I clear my throat and reach across the table to take Adrienne's hand. "This is my wife, Adrienne. And I'm Stew Rochard, by the way. That's my name."

The waitress groans and nods. "Okay. Very nice to meet you, and I apologize for blanking on that." She waves her order pad in the air. "I'll just get your order going and bring your coffee right over."

We watch her go, then Adrienne taps her foot against mine under the table. "Now who's being hit on?" she teases, smiling at me.

"What? No."

"Yes. That was a nerdy political version of what happened last night."

I give my a wife a long, disbelieving look, and she tips her head back and laughs. My phone vibrates, and I pull it out. It's an email I can reply to after I eat, so I put it away.

"At least with Gavin out west, I get you mostly to myself for breakfast," she says lightly.

I grunt. I don't like his unexpected trip. I don't like what I suspect is the reason behind it.

Adrienne doesn't miss any of my reaction, and her expression slides into serious concern. "Anything you can talk about?"

"Not really."

"Boo." She winks at me. She knows exactly how it is, and really doesn't mind. But at some point when we're alone I'm going to tell her that I worry the prime minister is falling head-over-heels in lust with the new intern, and there's no way that ends well.

"You make me extraordinarily happy, you know that?" I bracket her legs with mine under the table. "And at times like this, I'm grateful for what we have. I promise I know how much you've been carrying our family."

"So serious over breakfast," she murmurs, but she doesn't look away.

"I'm always serious about you. Have been since the first moment I laid eyes on you." She'd been a first year university student. I was an upper-year and tried to show off. Big man on campus. Hard to do with my tongue hanging out of my mouth.

She'd had my number from the start. "I remember."

I like the way her eyes go soft. "Good."

Our food arrives then, and we take our time, having a second cup of coffee before we finally settle the bill and head out on foot.

I swear Adrienne's disappointed that the waitress doesn't try to slip me her number when we leave. I take her hand. "What's next?"

We go to the Royal Ontario Museum for a temporary exhibit about tattoos from around the world. **Tattoos: Ritual. Identity. Obsession. Art** the brochure says. We wander through the quiet exhibit hall for an hour, some-times together and sometimes drifting apart. She takes my hand as we head upstairs to see dinosaur bones and leans in. "Remember when you wanted to get a tattoo?"

"Back in university?"

She winks at me. "Yeah."

It's at this point I realize two important things. First, my wife was long overdue for a weekend away, just the two of us. And second, deep down she's still that angsty rocker girl I fell in love with. Not so hidden at the moment.

She was more Guns N' Roses to my extensive Queen collection. I fell in love with her plaid shirts and Doc Martens, and kept that secret to myself until after I'd gone crazy for her clever mind and sexy mouth, too.

"I'm pretty sure I just said that to impress you." I curl a strand of her hair around my finger. "What did I want to get?"

"I don't remember. Probably something you'd hate now."

"We've changed a lot from back then, but…" I tug her close. "This is the same. This will always be the same."

Halfway up the wide, sweeping stairs of the Royal Ontario Museum, I kiss my wife, and it's not quick or discreet or polite. Life is too short for that. I make her breathless and I make her blush.

And that's exactly the same as it used to be, too.

6

ADRIENNE

OUR CHECK-OUT TIME at the hotel is noon. At ten minutes to, we're making out like teenagers in a fogged-up car, knowing curfew is about to crash down hard on us.

Hard being the operative word.

"What time is our train?" Stew asks, his voice rough as he slides his thigh between mine. His hands are everywhere, making me warm and distracted and trembly in the best way.

"In an hour. And I think the maid's going to come in here and start cleaning around us if we don't leave…" But I don't push him away. I want to soak up every last moment of privacy, too.

We spent most of yesterday outside, doing grown-up explore-the-city type things. We came back to the room for a sex-filled nap attempt before dinner, then headed out again. His phone rang three times, and he had a bunch of quick email breaks. But for the most part, work was out of sight and out of mind. And when he wasn't being dragged into urgent problems, I was the centre of his day and the object of all his attention.

It definitely refilled my well in more ways than one. Emotionally, sexually, adventurously…

And now we need to go home, because we have jobs and kids and a life. But we're going home together, and that's a gift, too.

"I had an amazing weekend," I whisper, brushing my lips along his jaw.

"I want to make rash promises about doing this again." Stew strokes my cheek, then lifts my chin with his knuckle so he can kiss me.

I open for him, curling my tongue against his, meeting him hungry stroke for hungry stroke. It's going to be ages until we can do this again. But that's on me as much as him. "Next time, I'll invite you along," I murmur. "And maybe we can do it in Ottawa, too."

He presses his erection into me. "Oh, we're doing it in Ottawa. Tonight."

"Not it. Well, yes, *it*. But this, I mean. We can get a room at the Chateau Laurier. You can stumble over to Zoe's Lounge after work and pick up the sexy mom in the hoodie at the bar."

"Tight t-shirt and Doc Martens."

"Or that."

"I love you in whatever you wear, and wherever you are."

I burrow close and breath in the scent of his skin. "I love you, too."

"I HATE YOU."

Stew grins at me as the train rattles towards Kingston. "What?"

I swallow hard and try to ignore his questing fingers along my thigh. "This is torture."

"I'm having fun."

"I bet you are." I stretch my legs out in front of me, trying to ignore how distractingly wet my panties are. In public.

On a *train*. With no hope of stripping them off and demanding my husband finish what he started for…I glance at my watch. Another two hours.

Great.

Part of me wants the prime minister to have another idea that needs urgent input from his chief of staff. A phone call or an email would distract Stew from his current mission of touching me, lightly and not-so-lightly, innocently and not-so-innocently, all over and as much as he can.

He started as soon as we pulled away from Union Station and he realized that our seats were private enough that nobody could actually see us unless they walked past us. So he turned toward me and drifted his fingertips along my collarbone before brushing my hair out of the way. "You're beautiful," he whispered against the curve of my ear.

Hot, right?

So hot.

Too hot, really. Because he didn't stop. By the time we stopped in Cobourg, I was warm and shifting in my seat. Belleville? I'd have agreed to whatever the train equivalent of the mile-high club is.

Now we're nearing Kingston and I'm crawling out of my skin. It turns out, you can be too turned on. That's a fun fact I wish I'd never learned.

"Go back to your book."

"No."

He laughs quietly. "Why not?"

"Because you keep reading over my shoulder and doing —" I lower my voice. "Whatever the hero does."

"He's got some great ideas."

I'm reading a Regency historical romance. There's a duke who is slowly seducing a governess. Stew latched on to the idea that I'm a governess of sorts, as a teacher, and he is, of course, the dashing duke.

He's certainly playing the rake card to perfection.

I snap open my book and resume reading.

So does he, and his hand continues its leisurely crawl from my knee to…oh, God. I turn the page. This isn't a scene that is going to end with a convenient mishap, ruining the duke's chance to get a little something something.

Unlike the governess, though, I'm not wearing voluminous skirts that hide wandering fingers.

I toss the book onto the opposite seat. "That's enough of that."

"You should have worn a skirt…" He sighs. "Opportunity lost."

"We can finish reading that scene together tonight when we go to bed."

"Oh, we will." He wraps his arm around me and tugs me close. "Now let me tell you a story I just thought up…"

WE TAKE a cab home from the train station. I haven't called about the kids yet, because I've been distracted, but real life dictates that we collect them soon—and a big part of me is keen to hear how their weekend was.

Another part of me wants to tie my husband to our bed first and teach him just how bossy my inner governess can be.

After we pay the cabbie, I fire off a deliberately vague text to my sister.

Adrienne: How's it going? Heading home.
Sandra: ETA? The boys just settled down with sand-wiches and a movie.

I glance at my husband, unlocking the front door to our house. The right thing to do here would be to tell the truth.

I do the opposite. It still feels right.

Adrienne: Should be home in an hour or so. Do you want us to come pick them up?
Sandra: I can bring them over. Hour-and-a-half sound good?

It sounds perfect.

"Who was that?" Stew asks as I hurry up the walk.

"Kid update. We've got ninety minutes to finish what you started on the train."

7

———————

STEW

I KNOW she thinks we need to rush, but as soon as Adrienne closes the front door, I take her bag from her hand and set it down. We're going to do this right, and we're going to do it slow.

"Now Miss Adrienne, whatever has you so worked up?"

She gives me an incredulous look. Incredulous, but aroused. Her cheeks are flushed and her eyes are bright. My dirty, delightful wife. "I am not an innocent governess and you are no rakish duke. Take off your clothes."

I ignore her and press her back against the wall, looming over her. "I love your bossy temper."

She reaches for my belt. "Fine, you can leave your clothes on."

Ha. I catch her wrists and pull her hands up between our bodies. "Nice try." I kiss her fingers. "An hour and a half, you say?"

She takes a deep, tormented breath and gives me a pleading look. "Yes."

"Do you think I'm terribly cruel?" I move on to the knuckles, nipping at them as she glowers at me.

"Uh, yeah."

I turn her wrist over so I can kiss the exposed, soft skin on the inside of her arm. "I can't help it, you know. You're too beautiful not to touch. To tease."

"But now we're alone," she whispers, sliding her hand out of my grasp and winding her arms around my neck. I let her. I'd let her do anything she wanted.

Almost anything.

She doesn't get to be in charge right now. I take her wrists and push them over her head, against the wall. "Exactly. We're alone. And awake. No kids. In our home. You want to know why I couldn't keep my hands off you on the train? Because I knew that for all the amazing sex we had this weekend, when I got you home, I'd get to make love to you. I thought it might be tonight, after you'd had to slide back into being mom, and I wanted you to hum all evening with the awareness of just how much I want you."

Something bright flashes in her eyes. Excitement, maybe, but something else, too.

I lean down and drag my lips along her jaw. "We don't need to escape from reality," I say roughly as I breathe her in. "I want you just as much, here."

She exhales quickly. Relief. That's the something else I'd seen in her eyes, and can feel rolling off her body now as she presses against me. "Same."

I hold her there, my reluctant prisoner, while I trace my fingers down her body and tease them under the hem of her shirt. She's soft and delicious. I move my hand back up again, this time under the fabric, against her skin. I find her bra and cover the swell of her breast with my palm, not missing that her nipple is pulled tight already, a hard nub that must send jolts of awareness to her core as I rub against it.

More than twenty-five years we've been doing this, and

I'll never tire of that sex-glazed look in her eye, the way she goes soft and wanting when I work her up. Sure, I teased her on the train, but this is something else. This is foreplay with intent. So much intent.

I watch her melt for me. I imagine heat stoking inside her, turning her liquid from the inside out, and I amp up my touches. Firmer, brusquer. I pinch her nipple now, through the fabric of her bra, and she gasps.

Music to my ears.

I cover her mouth with mine, swallowing her desperate pleas for more. I kiss her until a primal need to take my wife—hard, fast, and so thoroughly she can't walk for a while—is thudding in my veins.

Wrenching myself away from her, I grab her hips and pivot us both, pointing her toward the stairs. "Up you go."

She scampers ahead of me and I follow, once again unable to keep my hands off her.

In our room, she moves to close the door behind us.

"Leave it open," I tell her, and she gives me a wide-eyed, disbelieving look.

I don't know why it matters, but it does.

She swallows hard, but doesn't say anything. She doesn't close the door, either.

"If they come home, the front door is locked. We'll hear them better this way." Lies. I like the element of danger way more than I'm being a sensible father right now.

Her eyes light up, knowing. She sees me to my core, my wife does. She licks her lips. "You'd like it if I had to suddenly be quiet, wouldn't you?"

"I'd hate it," I growl as I nudge her onto the bed. "Because it would mean we've been interrupted, and I very much want to wring you out completely before the kids come home."

I fall on top of her, being careful not to be too heavy as I fit us together. Still too many clothes in between. I peel her shirt up as she fumbles with my belt. We roll sideways in a tangle of limbs and clothes, until we're both naked and I'm between her thighs, my cock jutting up against her belly as I kiss her again.

Never enough kisses.

Never enough time.

So much to pour into forty-five hours. Too much to say and words are definitely inadequate.

One last attempt to show her everything she means to me before this window of opportunity, this gift of time, closes.

She curls her legs around me as I work my way down her body, until my hands are full of her breasts and my face is buried in the sweet valley between them. I nuzzle her there, where her skin is sensitive and I know it'll make her shiver. Then I lick my way over the field of delicious goose-bumps on her skin, tasting every inch of her breasts before I reach her tight, ready nipple.

Ready for me to circle, to tease.

Ready for me to swallow, to pulse against my tongue as I suck on her flesh.

My wife.

She reaches between us, and I let her capture my erec-tion with her clever, knowing fingers. She strokes me with a familiarity that makes my knees weak. Her thumb rolls over the sensitive head, flared and swollen and wet at the tip. I grow harder still. I'm so ready, but I want her on fire before I take her. I want her so hot that I can be rough, that she'll need me to be that for her.

And in return, she can set me ablaze, too. Consume me with her heat and her beauty. I'll thunder into her and she'll wrap around me, taking every last inch.

I duck my head to her other breast, loving that nipple

with my mouth, my tongue, my teeth, until she's squirming beneath me, trying to bring us together.

I smooth my hand over her thigh, opening her wide for my touch. Her curls are slick, that's how wet she is for me, and inside, she's hot and soft and grippy as I give her first one, then two fingers.

"Now," she breathes, and I'm not going to argue with that.

Even after a weekend of fucking, the first press feels like there's no way I'll fit inside her. I always do. She's perfect for me. I just need to work for it. She throws her head back and groans in delight at the intrusion. The horny, happy sound only makes me thicker.

She wiggles beneath me, rolling her hips as we work together to get me deep inside her. Each pulse is wet and warm, like tongues against my cock. Like I've got a dozen Adriennes all worshipping my dick, and how do I keep control at an image like that?

I can't. No way.

I hold her still as I piston my hips, rocking all the way into her. She cries out my name, then whispers, "Again, do it again."

I push her hands above her head, our fingers linked. All of me presses against all of her as I thrust into her again. No chance of being careful now. I'm heavy and hard and demanding as I take her right to the edge, as I make her tremble and shake for me.

"Fuck." That's what I'm reduced to, single word, guttural curses.

But she's right there with me in the sex-drunk haze. I feel her lips on my neck, then her tongue.

Blackness starts to crowd at the corners of my vision as I plow into her. Savage, desperate rutting. I can feel her tightening up, clutching at me inside and her limbs tensing too. As if she were actually climbing toward that figurative peak.

"Come for me," I say roughly. The headboard slaps against the wall and we both reach for it, pushing it into the wall in a desperate attempt to not wake anyone up.

Oh, how conditioned we are.

But we're alone.

We can make as much noise as we want. I reach between us and cup her breast, catching her nipple between my fingers.

"Oh, yes!" She grinds against me as I bury myself inside her, holding still because I'm so fucking close to exploding and that can't happen until— "Jesus, yes. Stew. God. I'm coming!"

I thrust again, losing myself inside her pussy.

My. Fucking. Wife.

"Love you," I say, my voice ragged as I brace my arms on either side of her.

She kisses me, her breath coming hard and fast. "Me, too. Okay. That was worth the wait."

And we still have time to share a shower.

STEW

The RETURN to work is a brutal, unforgiving return to reality.

Gavin has decided to stay in Vancouver all week, which pisses me off because work is piling up. We're all working longer days since his work day out west doesn't end until well after dark in Ottawa. Whenever he wants to get his head sorted out straight and get his ass back here, that will make me happy. Until then, I do the best I can.

Ellie is working like mad on a communications strategy around donors and fundraising. I like what she comes up with, and I tell her as much. She's done a lot under harsh constraints, because I don't want her to give any hint of Gavin's new direction to the party activists planning his next event.

By Friday, Gavin signs off on the plan, too, and even better, he decides to come back to the capital.

Finally.

The relief I feel is so palpable, I'm sure he can sense it across the country.

I send the entire office an email ordering them to go

home to their families, friends, roommates, cats, or house plants.

I don't care where they go, I just don't want anyone to stay late.

I know I'm not going to be at work after six. It might be the last chance any of us have for a few weeks to have a bit of a personal life, and my family—my wife especially—deserves me to seize that opportunity.

My entire day is oriented around getting out the door at quarter to six.

I manage to leave at five to the hour.

It'll have to be good enough.

When I get home, the twins are skateboarding in the dead-end at the bottom of our street. I wave to them and head inside, where I find my oldest and my wife in a silent standoff of sorts in the kitchen.

I give Adrienne a look to ask, *what's going on?*

She just shrugs.

I take a deep breath. "What's for dinner?"

Adrienne points to the fridge. "Steaks are ready to go on the grill. I've got the potatoes almost ready, too. And a salad."

"Your favourite," Daniel says sullenly from behind his cell phone.

I sit on the bar stool next to him and nab the device from his hands.

"Hey!"

"Hey, what?" I keep my voice light.

"I was using that."

"I could tell. Whatever you were doing, it can wait a minute. Look at me."

It takes him a while, but his eyes finally flick up to meet my gaze. "What?"

He thinks he's going to get in trouble, when really, it's

me that needs a talking to. "I'm sorry I've been missing a lot of dinners."

He shrugs. "Whatever."

"No. Not whatever. It's not ideal. But it's also not permanent, and I'd appreciate you not making your mom's life that much harder just because I'm being an ass—"

"Okay, who wants to set the table?" Adrienne calls out, her voice unnecessarily loud.

Daniel cracks a smile and winks at me. "Don't say ass in front of Mom, she doesn't like it," he whispers.

"Right," I whisper back. "I forgot."

He swivels off his stool and yanks open the cutlery drawer.

Adrienne waits until he's grabbed forks for everyone and headed to the dining room before smiling at me. "Bonding through bad language?"

"Whatever works." I get up and reach past her, opening the cupboard. I stop to give her a quick kiss. "Thanks for having faith in me."

"Always." She sighs. "Why is it so easy for you with him?"

"It's not. That was just a brief reprieve. And he pushes harder against you because he knows he can. Because he knows you're our rock, and you're not going anywhere."

Her eyes soften as she leans into me. "You're not going anywhere, either."

"I need to do a better job of showing them that." I kiss the top of her head. "Can I grill?"

"Please."

"Give me five minutes to change out of my work stuff."

She pats my ass. "Go put on those tight jeans from last weekend. Give me a thrill."

"Mom!" From the doorway, Daniel covers his eyes as he

howls about how gross it is that his parents touch each other.

An unforgiving return to reality, indeed.

I give Adrienne a light kiss on the lips. I wouldn't have it any other way.

THE END

INTERESTED IN GAVIN and Ellie's story? A kinky Prime Minister, a vanilla intern, and a scandal that shouldn't feel so right or cost so much. *Prime Minister* is available now, and you can read the first five chapters now by turning the page! You can also find all the ebook links on our website:

www.friskybeavers.com

While you're there, be sure to sign up for our new release alert because the next Frisky Beavers book is right around the corner!

~ Ainsley & Sadie

AN EXCERPT FROM PRIME MINISTER

Gavin:

Ellie Montague is smart, sensitive, and so gorgeous it hurts to look at her. She's also an intern in my office. The office of the Prime Minister of Canada.*

That's me. The PM.

She calls me that because when she calls me *Sir* I get hard and she gets flustered, and as long as she's my intern, I can't twist my hands in her strawberry-blonde hair and show her what else I'd like her to do with that pretty pink mouth.**

Ellie:

How much I like the PM varies on a daily basis. He's intense, controlling, and a perfectionist in every way—and he demands the same of his staff.

How much I want him never wavers.

There's something about him that tugs at me deep inside, and makes me wish that just once he'd cross the line in a late night work session. I'd take that secret to the grave if it meant I got a taste of the barely restrained beast inside him.***

FOOTNOTES:

* This is a fictional erotic romance. No prime ministers or interns were harmed in the making of this book.

** Except it's a BDSM romance, so they were hurt a little.

*** Spoiler alert: she gets more than a taste. And she likes it.

1

ELLIE

THE ONLY THING worse than being late for your first day of work is when your first day of work is at the Parliament Buildings and your new boss is the prime minister.

Who you have a secret crush on, except it doesn't need to be a secret, because he's single and hot and every other woman in the country also has a crush on him.

You could wear a placard that says **I want to bang the PM** and nobody would even notice, because they would all be wearing variations on the same theme.

Of course, it should be a secret because I'm going to be working for him.

With him.

Under him.

Stop it, Ellie.

It's only a three month internship, and technically there's a deputy director of communications and a chief of staff between us in the chain of command. But my nipples don't understand that and they're super excited about working so closely with Gavin.

Mr. Strong.

Like every other straight woman, gay man, or anyone in the middle of the Kinsey scale, I've got a crush on the man. Which is why I should have been early for work, and is also why I'm running late.

I should have been focused on making a good impression.

Instead, I'd changed my outfit three times and chose heels that made it impossible to hustle when I realized just how late I was.

I squeak in the front doors at 7:59 by the clock on my cell phone. But of course there's a security line to get through and—

"Ms. Montague?"

I'd recognize that voice anywhere. Thick with humour, warm and rough enough at the edges to appeal to steel workers and farmers—that was the panty-melting voice of our nation's brand new prime minister.

I know that voice.

Until this moment, I had no clue he might know me.

So I stare at him dumbly.

This is not my finest hour.

"Sir," I finally stammer out.

The women behind me in line giggle.

That's the effect this man has on people. I'm now officially blocking the security line into the building and nobody cares because Gavin Strong, The Honourable Prime Minister of Canada, is flashing his baby blue eyes at everyone in a thirty foot radius. He's done this before—stop and talk to his staff on the way in, but I'm still flustered. I don't think I ever expected to talk to him, and definitely not before my first day has even begun.

"Shall we head inside?"

"Yes, of course." I yank out my wallet. "I'll see you in there."

He holds my gaze for a moment, probably a second or two, but it's the kind of second that stretches. Long enough to be meaningful for me but nothing for him.

And then he's turning, shaking hands with the people in front of me. Welcoming them all to work today.

Who does that?

Gavin Strong. Union lawyer, community activist, Habitat for Humanity volunteer. The most personable man in the entire country, possibly the smartest, too, although he likes to play that bit down.

Surround himself with experts, he says.

That's where I come in.

I'm hardly an expert, but I'm getting there. Bachelor's degree in Women's Studies and Sociology. Master's in Women's Studies. One year into my doctorate, which is loosely a business degree but specifically a communications specialty.

And I've scored one of ten brand-new internships with the federal government. Cultural Change Officers, we're called. I've taken a three-month leave of absence from my studies to do this job.

To work under the prime minister.

And I didn't make it three minutes into the role without my panties getting wet.

Fan-fucking-tastic.

IT TAKES five hours for my crush to die a miserable death.

Gavin might be hot, and smart, but he's also a perfectionist, and he expects that of his staff. Which is fine for me, because I haven't pissed him off yet, but by lunch I've witnessed enough to know that if I don't lock down my libido and bring my A-game, I'm going to get called on the carpet.

The showdown he had midmorning with his Chief of Staff—Stew Rochard, my boss—over fundraising and lobbyists has the entire office in a panic, because we've got a private event in five weeks that might need to be cancelled if the PM decides to take a hard line on influencers.

That's how I've decided I need to think about Gavin. The PM. The Prime Minister.

I'm not going to notice how good he looks in a suit or how his powerful thighs are outlined every time he sits down. The suit represents the position. It demands my respect, nothing else.

Instead of taking me out to lunch for my first day, Stew gives me half of the ham and Swiss on rye that his wife made him, digs two cans of Diet Coke out of a box he keeps under his desk, and tasks me with figuring out how we can spin the $5,000 a plate dinner into something that won't offend our boss quite so much.

Because I'm a freak for these kinds of problems, this makes me happy. A nice lunch would probably be nothing but small talk, and I'm kind of awkward when it comes to that. Like I should have asked Stew about his wife and kids when he gave me the sandwich, but I was already poring over the file on the fundraiser—the history of it, the host, the criticism on the other events that led to the PM's edict two hours earlier that we would *not* be in the pockets of the wealthy.

"One problem with him saying that over and over again is that he's rich, too," I point out as I lick mustard off my fingers. "And everyone knows it. Don't get me wrong—most people like that about him. But he's hardly one of us with the sandwiches from home."

Stew snorts. "Don't let him hear you say that."

"He's a man of the people in many other ways. He knows how much a loaf of bread costs, that's all that matters. But he's also comfortable with these donors, right? What if it wasn't a fundraiser for the party? What if it was...like a kick-off for a community challenge?"

"Keep talking." He roots around in his lunch bag. "Chocolate chip cookie?"

I shake my head. "But I'll take another pop if you've got one."

"He shouldn't shut himself off from business leaders. He needs to stay connected to them, and show them who's boss. Canadians just want to know that he's not in their pockets. They'll be thrilled if he can turn it around, make them bend to his will."

"Shit." He rocks back in his chair and shoves the rest of his cookie in his mouth. "That's good."

The truth is, it's not a new idea. It was a critique I wrote six months earlier for a class, as a response to a hypothetical case study that was eerily similar. I got lucky on my first day, but I'm smart enough to pretend that my luck is actually talent. "Thanks."

"It'll need some work. You'll need to present it with the repercussions forecasted out in all directions."

"Of course." I've done that at school before, too. If I've got time, I'll tap a couple of my profs and get their—

"I want you to pitch it tomorrow in the morning briefing."

Oh, crap. So no time, then. "Tomorrow. Right."

"That a problem?"

"No."

Stew opens his mouth, maybe to warn me about what the PM expects, or maybe to question how sure I am, I don't know, because before he can say anything, in whirls a six-foot-three-inch hurricane wearing a suit and righteous indignation.

"This report from the Ministry of the Environment is fucking bullshit, Stewart," the PM growls as he storms in from the hallway.

Stew doesn't miss a beat. "I'm in a meeting, Gavin."

The PM's gaze swings around to where I'm sitting. "Ms. Montague. Would you step outside?"

My immediate reaction is yes, of course. But that's the wrong answer.

That's the woman inside me doing what a man has asked of her, because he doesn't want to make her feel uncomfortable.

Seriously? Fuck that noise. "I'd rather stay."

He gives me a hard, unreadable look.

"Sir," I add, swallowing hard. "I'd rather stay, sir."

His eyes flash in surprise and anger, and my palms go all sweaty.

"Because…I'm the barometer, right? Without me, you're talking in an echo chamber. That's what you said in your announcement about these internships." I turn to my boss. "I don't think your office is an echo chamber, of course, Stew."

Gavin chuckles, an unexpected sound after a day that's felt beyond tense. "No, Stew has no problem telling me when I'm wrong."

I take a deep breath. "Neither will I. Sir."

He gives me another long look, this one more compli-cated, but just as hard to read.

Finally he nods. "But stop calling me sir. That's my father's name."

His father's name is Vince, but I get the point. "Okay. So what part of the report is fucking bullshit?"

He laughs and turns back to Stew. "This one can stay."

2

GAVIN

BY TEN O'CLOCK THIS MORNING, my day had completely derailed—not an unusual situation. Twice my assistant Beth quietly suggested that we change our estimated arrival time at the City Farm Camp. There's a press conference at five thirty, after the kids have left for the day. I only need to be there for an hour beforehand to get a tour and have a photo op with some of the children.

But I'm only three months into my first term as PM. I'm not interested in doing the bare minimum. I've heard amazing things about this program, and we've got a plan to greatly expand the tax credits and subsidies for ones just like it across the country.

I'm not going to talk about that without actually spending some real time with the kids and the counsellors.

Plus, horses and sheep and chickens. What's not to love about that? It's certainly more fun than a bullshit environmental report that completely misses the mark—

I cut myself off. I'm not going to get worked up about it. The delightful Ellie Montague is going to tear into that report and tell me all the ways we can render it null and void, and justify spending the money on a new one.

I need to have Substantive Fucking Policy tattooed on all deputy ministers' foreheads, clearly.

I've just finished the most intellectually stimulating conversation I've had in weeks in Stew's office, with Ellie… Ellie, who I can't get off my mind.

Dangerous territory, I tell myself. I don't listen. There's something about her that fires me up in a long-dormant way.

"It's two o'clock," Beth says as she strides into my office. She's going to try again to rearrange my day.

"You haven't had a chance to return these four calls yet," she says smoothly, sliding a call sheet on top of the report I was just about to open. *Reading time is over*—her message is clear.

I give her a side-eye and she just smiles sweetly at me.

Beth. She's like the sister I already have. Between her and Pia, my actual sister, I don't get cut any slack. So Beth is like the baby sister I never had, and when she's not riding my ass about the damn itinerary, I like her a lot. Even the bossy parts.

She's adjusted amazingly well to the new role. I hired her on my first day in the city as an MP two years ago, and everyone said she was too young and inexperienced to be the executive assistant to a national leader. Everyone was wrong. She's my secret weapon for keeping a tight schedule —every day except today.

Today, I'm going to camp whether she likes it or not.

She doesn't.

Oh well.

I grab the call sheet and wave it at her. "You sure you don't want to come with me?"

She gives me a look of great alarm. "To muck out barns?"

"Yeah."

"No. Make those calls or I'm coming to find you later! Remember I can see who you call on your cell phone."

Yeah. That's why I have two phones. The official phone of the Prime Minister of Canada, and the burner phone I use to call my best friend, Max, when this all gets to be a little too surreal.

As I hop in the back of my armoured town car, I think this should be one of the times I call him. But I've got four phone calls to make in a thirty minute drive to the Agriculture Museum, and I have a certain doctoral candidate to do a little more research on, too.

Ellie Montague.

I try to tell myself that my interest is purely professional. She's smart and capable and she's only on loan to us for three months from the University of Ottawa. If she's impressing Stew on her first day of the job, we need to be amping up her responsibilities while she's here.

But first, phone calls.

CAMP IS in fact more fun than reading reports or even fighting with Stew.

I find myself wondering if Ellie likes animals, and shove that thought away as fast as it pops into my head.

The most amazing discovery about the camp I make this afternoon is what a difference the experience makes for kids who are struggling in school. So, after I spend nearly three hours being taught by children how to care for the animals and manage the other farm chores, I get a little pissed off when the first question I get from the press is about how much my shirt cost—because it's now smeared with mud.

"I'm going to be lucky if that's mud. Pretty sure I got that when we were mucking out the horse stalls," I tell Rick Stupes, a reporter with CAN News who is always out to make me look like Richie Rich. I don't respond to the rest of his question because it's stupid.

He tries again. "When your staff set up this photo op up, did they advise you to wear anything different?"

Seriously, what is this guy's problem? I'm only slightly more GQ than the last guy.

Okay, no, I'm a thousand times more GQ than the last guy.

I kick my foot out from behind the podium. "I've been wearing these boots since I left the house at half past five this morning, because I'm not a toddler, and I know how to dress myself appropriately. As a side note, they're the boots I hiked Golden Ears in after we won the most recent election." Take that, Rick. "Nobody had to remind me to put them on. Coming to City Farm Camp has been the highlight of a difficult week, something I've really been looking forward to, and if I didn't have a full day of work tomorrow, I'd be back in a heartbeat."

The next question is similarly off-topic. Inside my head, I'm calling the press corps all sorts of names, but we've practised this over and over again. My natural propensity to snap at stupid people is well and truly beaten out of me now. Or at least well internalized.

I smile and give a short answer. Rinse and repeat, until the fifth question gets to the heart of the announcement I've just made, about funding for such activities needing to be a two-fisted approach, because not all parents can wait for a tax credit to justify the upfront expense.

And sometimes, those are the kids who need the alternative learning experience the most.

I smoothly reiterate what the camp director has already said, about how the hands-on care of animals instills empathy and compassion that translates well back to human interaction.

I know as soon as I finish the spiel, with an extra charming smile for the reporter who asked the right question, that's the clip that'll run on the news.

We don't always nail it this well, but when we do, it makes the rest of it worthwhile.

ELLIE

I DON'T LEAVE the office until after eight. I only stumble as far as a sushi restaurant three blocks away, where my roommate, Sasha, is waiting for me.

"That bad?" she asks, flagging down the waitress. "We're going to need sake."

"No sake. Green tea. And then I'm hitting the last yoga class of the night."

"Ew."

"I'm not making you come with me."

Sasha's a runner. Uptight, controlled…she's practically allergic to finding her resting place and just breathing.

Me? I'm spastic, anxious, and a chronic worrier. I hold it all at bay by doing yoga five days a week.

Not usually this late at night, but hello real world. I've been spoiled by being a grad student—it's hard work, but I can mostly do it on my own schedule.

Not anymore.

I have to be back at work at six thirty tomorrow morning. Tell the PM he's wrong at seven. Then probably fight with people all day as I convince them I'm right. If I don't centre myself and get a good night's sleep, that's not going to go well.

67

with people all day as I convince them I'm right. If I don't centre myself and get a good night's sleep, that's not going to go well.

4

GAVIN

THE FIRST THING I notice when my senior team files into my office for our daily briefing at seven is Ellie Montague. This doesn't surprise me, because I haven't been able to stop thinking about her since yesterday. She looks tired and my imagination takes off in search of a likely explanation. Most of them involve her being kept up all night by a man. Narrowing down her type was proving problematic. She didn't seem like she'd go for the muscle-bound studly type with more balls than brains, but I've been surprised more than a few times by what can get a woman wet and needy.

I watch her from the corner of my eye as Stew talks to my staff—his staff—about what's come up overnight, what our priorities are for the day, and a number of other things that he doesn't need me to listen to. Which is good, because I'm too busy cataloguing all the ways she fascinates me. What I notice most is Ellie's fidgeting. She keeps catching herself, and I find it hard not to smirk.

She smooths the front of her skirt with her hand and leaves behind a long streak slightly darker than the khaki fabric. Her palms are sweaty. She's nervous. I barely have time to wonder why when Stew invites her to speak.

Her head comes up at the sound of her name and our gazes lock for a moment, then she drops her clear grey eyes to the binder she's holding in her shaking hands. I'm glad I'm sitting down because I'm pretty sure waving my raging hard-on around the room is not on the briefing agenda.

I watch her lips as they form the words I'm not really hearing because I'm busy imaging what they would feel like on my cock.

I should be paying more attention to what she's saying, but I already know I'm going to agree with whatever plan she's laying out.

She wouldn't be speaking right now if Stew wasn't already going to back her recommendations on how to keep these outrageously expensive rubber chicken dinners that are supposed to be party fundraisers from becoming opportunities for big business to buy some private time with the prime minister. Pay to play, they call it.

Confident this embarrassing little hiccup is already handled, I drift back into my fantasy. Something I shouldn't be doing for so many reasons, not the least of which is she's young enough to be my niece.

But I can't help myself.

She's on her back, draped over my desk with her head tipped back over one edge, her legs dangling over the other.

I unzip my trousers and free my long-suffering erection.

"Open," I demand.

Her lips part and I trace them with the tip of my cock until they're glossy with pre-come. I want to be rough, make her take me all the way down, but for some unknown reason, I hold myself back. Her tongue swirls around the head as I slide in.

The sight of my fluid smeared all over her lips makes me want to mark her other places. Her tits, her back, her ass.

As I slip farther into her hot, eager mouth, I take her hands, weaving our fingers together. I hold them against the surface of the desk and lean forward, stopping just above her mound of soft red curls. In my fantasy they're a bit darker than the strawberry blonde waves I've seen her twist her fingers into more than once.

She's ethereal and bright. Impish and totally captivating. "Spread your legs, Sprite."

I slide out and in with shallow strokes as I move my head lower so I can tickle at her clit with my tongue. She squirms and I stop.

"Don't move."

Curious to see how much she can take, I push my cock in until it barely touches the back of her throat. Her belly lurches a little, but she swallows against it. Her mouth is hot and wet and tight around me, and I want her to take even more but I won't push her. Not the first time.

"Good girl," I say. Because she is. I resume my shallow thrusts into her mouth and lower myself back down to feast on her pussy.

This time she stays perfectly still while I suck and lick at her clit. I catch that firm nub between my lips and tug gently. She struggles to keep still and I get a thrill from her obedience.

While I'm consumed with her delightful pussy, she's working away on my cock. Even with the position of her head restricting her movement, she does an excellent job of giving me all the suction and friction I need to get me where I want to go. She's gotta come first, but her mouth is unbelievable. Distracting.

Fuck, I want to rut against her and let myself go, but I can't.

I concentrate harder on my goal. She starts to moan and—

Ellie's lips stop moving and I'm yanked back to reality. Not that I was all that far away. I may have been having wildly inappropriate fantasies about my Chief of Staff's far-too-young-for-me intern, but I was present enough to keep from making a complete fool of myself.

"Thank you for your presentation, Ellie. I'll take it under advisement." Stew gives me the look. The one that says I am going to have some explaining to do. And I am going to have to do some fast thinking, because I sure as shit won't tell him the real reason my mind wasn't where it should be.

"Okay everybody, I think that's everything for today." Stew gestures towards the door, but doesn't exit with the rest of the group.

I watch as Ellie leaves. Damn that skirt looks good on her from the front, but it hugs her ass tight, and the rear view is spectacular.

The last person is barely out of the room before Stew shuts the door.

There are only two men in the entire world who know me for who I really am. Who would watch me in that briefing and see where my mind really went. One of them is safely on the other side of the country living his own life.

The other is standing in front of me, trying his damnedest to keep *my* life on track.

Stew shakes his head. "What the fuck got into you?"

I haven't thought fast enough and I'm saved from having to give an excuse by his ire, because he's already worked up and intent on pointing out how much of an ass I just was.

"That girl was working all night because yesterday at lunch I told her to have that presentation ready for this morning's briefing. The least you could have fucking done, you inconsiderate piece of shit, was listen to her proposal. Instead, you had your head up your ass thinking about God only knows what, and I don't want to know."

I wince. "Was I that obvious?"

"Only to me. You've got to come up with a new phrase when you mentally return to meetings because it won't be long before others will figure out *I'll take it under advisement* means my brain had more important matters than whatever twaddle you're peddling."

"Twaddle?"

"Gavin, it was her first briefing. She was nervous and you were unbelievably rude. And that's not like you."

"You're right. I should apologise."

"Nah, she was too nervous to notice you were being an asshat. I think you'll do more damage than good by drawing attention to it."

"Are you sure?"

"You're willing to blindly accept my recommendations when it comes to how we deal with this fundraiser business, but on something as trivial as this, you question my wisdom?"

"Fuck, Stew. How did I even get here? Two years ago I was happily spanking shitty employers for mistreating their workers and now I'm running the fucking country."

"Not for much longer if you don't keep your head in the game. What if that had been Question Period instead of your morning briefing?"

He's right and I know it. "Point taken. Now, don't you have work to do?"

Stew shoots me his middle finger and walks out the door.

I lean back in my chair and prop my feet on my desk, crossing them at the ankles. The same desk I'd just been—

Fuck. I need to get laid. This dry spell is completely fucking with my judgement.

And I need to stop thinking about Ellie Montague's ass. Her mouth. How pink her pussy will be when she's wet and swollen for me.

Most of all, I need to stop finding her fidgeting so damn endearing.

5

—————

ELLIE

By Saturday, I'm totally ready for the weekend.

Except Stew emails me at six in the morning and I end up working until noon. There are a few people in the office, but everyone is heads down on their own stuff. I'm in and out in five hours, and I've still got two days of down time to enjoy.

Okay, so I'll get a day and a half. Maybe a day and a quarter, because there's some serious reading I need to do tomorrow night to be ready for Monday morning.

But a day off still sounds heavenly. Yoga, brunch, lying on the couch like a vegetable and watching something on Netflix. I can squeeze all of that into a day and a quarter. Maybe brunch can be something delivered and easily consumed while lying on the couch.

I check the yoga studio's schedule. My favourite teacher has a class at three today and another at seven tomorrow morning. That is not happening, so this afternoon it is.

I change out of my work clothes and pull on red yoga pants, a bralette with fancy braided straps, and a floaty black scoop-neck t-shirt that falls off one shoulder and shows off the twisted black and red fabric. I'll pull it off when I get to yoga, but I'm not so one-with-my-body that I'll walk to the studio in a top that anyone outside of the studio would see as a bra.

I'm halfway there when my phone pings again.

I wince as I check it.

Another email from Stew. Apparently getting lucky and proving myself helpful in the first week has consequences.

No good deed goes unpunished. Or…I'm establishing a reputation in a city where I want to have a long and productive career. I take a deep breath. The environmental report on the pipeline needs to be read from a youth jobs perspective. Can I have some thoughts for him by Monday?

I can, and I will, but I need the report, which can't be transmitted electronically yet. Crap.

So much for yoga. I glance at the clock on my phone screen. Quarter after two.

A gentle screech of bus brakes behind me makes the decision easy. It's a quick trip up the street. I can get to the office, get the report, and get back here in time for class. I spin around and wave my bus pass at the driver.

Twelve minutes later, I'm sprinting past the security guards, who laugh at me because I was already there once and it's Saturday and ha ha ha, not funny.

New girl is trying to make a good impression, okay?

Upstairs, pretty much everyone is gone. I let myself into the office I share with a couple of other junior staffers and grab the confidential report from the locked cabinet beneath my desk. The cover is stiff, though, and I need it to roll up so it will fit into my yoga mat bag.

Stew's copy has a floppy cover. I head to his office, but I can't find his copy anywhere. Frustrated, I check my phone. I'm not making that yoga class. Maybe I'll go to the one at four, even though the instructor is way too obsessed with the sound of her own voice for it to be truly Zen.

Then I call my boss. "Stew, I'm standing in your office. Where would I find your copy of the environmental report?"

"What's wrong with your copy?"

It won't fit in my yoga mat bag probably isn't the right answer. But it's the only one I've got, so I tell him the truth.

It takes him a while to stop laughing, so I lean on his desk and consider just taking a nap there like that, bent right over.

Once he stops laughing and tells me where to find it on his bookshelf, I say a muffled thanks and hang up the phone.

I don't get up right away.

It's been a really long week.

I groan and mumble to myself, "Might just stay here for a while."

"Are we working you that hard, Ms. Montague?" a voice asks from the doorway. A rich, warm voice with a now familiar-in-person rough edge to it.

The PM.

And I'm sprawled across my boss's desk in yoga pants and a bra. Kind of wearing a t-shirt, but when you're in front of the nation's leader, does *kind of* count?

No, no it does not.

"Sir," I gasp, pushing myself upright, suddenly aware that my ass was just in the air.

"I thought I told you not to call me that," he says.

I spin around and he's looking at the floor, and then the shelves, and finally his gaze settles on a point just past my shoulder.

That's weird, because he's usually such an eye-contact kind of guy. And it makes me self-conscious, like, he was also aware that my ass had been in the air, and is now behind me, but the rest of me is still clad in yoga wear.

And normally, this is not a big deal. I didn't think twice of wearing it in front of the security guards, for example.

But after a week of trying very hard to not be aware of the PM as a man, and at the same time being rather painfully aware that he is a man, with eyes, and…

All of that.

Sigh.

He's not the person I want to be standing in front of in skin-tight cropped yoga pants.

I'm not even wearing underwear under them, and I swear he's got Superman's X-ray vision right now, which is why he's *not* looking at me. Because he already did and he saw under my clothes and oh God, I need to work under him for another two months and three weeks.

With him.

I really need to stop making that slip inside my head. One of these days I'm going to say it out loud and everyone will know that I'm thinking about how big he is and how heavy he would feel on top of me.

While all this is rioting through my head and he's waiting for me to say something, *not* looking at me, I consider hiding behind Stew's chair to remove the inappropriate clothing from being a factor. But at some point he's going to expect me to leave this office, so I just stand where I am, suddenly feeling very, very naked.

Naked and slowly turning red.

"My apologies. I was just here to get…" Something I can't remember. Luckily the PM doesn't have that problem.

"The environmental report. I heard. Stew keeps his on the bookshelf." He clears his throat and points behind me. "Over there."

"Right." I turn and look at the second shelf.

"Next one up, I think."

I push up on my toes, because I'm short and Stew is not. Yeah, I can't reach.

"Here," Gavin says, and he's right behind me now. My pulse is jackhammering away in my neck. I can hear it in my ears. Can he hear it? It's loudly pronouncing my lascivious thoughts. The arm of his suit jacket brushes my bare skin as his hand reaches easily past mine and grabs the stack of nearly identical confidential reports.

How many of those does my boss get in a week? I only have the one to read. Suddenly my whining about my workload seems to lack perspective.

I turn and press my back against the bookshelf as he flips through the stack, finding the one I need.

"Here you go." He hands it over, and I press it to my chest as he leans over me to put the rest of the stack away again.

He's taller up close. I have to tip my head back to look up at him. Of course, I usually wear heels, and the canvas slip-ons I wear to yoga have zero lift.

"Thank you," I breathe, about to add *sir* when I catch myself. He laughs as he watches me form the start of the word, then press my lips together.

"Gavin. You can call me Gavin."

"I'm pretty sure I can't," I laugh, turning my head to the side in embarrassment.

"You need to, because this *sir* thing is killing us both and it's only been a week." He steps back and taps his index finger to his bottom lip. "Let's practise."

"Really?"

"Yes, really. Try... 'Hey, Gavin, how's your weekend going?'"

"Hey...Gavin." That feels weird. And nice, kind of, but

mostly weird and possibly dangerous because his eyes are extra blue right now.

He laughs, his shoulders shaking silently at what I can only assume is the dorkiest look on my face, but it breaks the ice. I square my shoulders and give him a stern look. He cocks one eyebrow and sobers his mouth. "Keep going."

"How's your weekend going?"

"Ah, you know. Had to work on Saturday."

"Me too." This is actually working. It's fun to talk to him like he's a regular person and not someone who overwhelms me at every turn. "Well, part of it, anyway. I tried to go to yoga."

His eyes twinkle as he follows my lead. "What happened?"

"Got stuck at the office."

"Bummer."

"It was okay. I almost got a mini nap on my boss's desk. But then I got busted by his boss, which was awkward."

"Sounds awful."

I grin. "Not so bad, actually."

"Phew."

I wiggle the report in the air between us. "Thank you, again. And I'm going to get out of your hair now, so you can get on with that mythical weekend thing."

He gestures his hand gallantly toward the door. "After you."

He's standing in front of my yoga mat. I point to it. "I just need…"

Instead of moving, he reaches down and grabs it. When he hands it over, his fingers brush mine, and I'm reminded again why everyone and their brother falls in love with this man.

There's definitely something about him, a heat that's

impossible to resist, but safe at the same time. It's super sexy, and my breath stutters on the inhale.

His gaze drops to my mouth, and when he looks back up at my eyes, the heat's gone, like he's purposefully made himself cold inside toward me, and after the stupid teasing conversation about names, I've gotta say it's unexpected.

It reminds me that I'm underdressed and overexposed, especially when it comes to my reactions to him.

He doesn't want me perving on him.

Nobody would. It's not professional. But before I can apologize, he's muttering a goodbye and on his way down the hall.

I follow slowly, pausing at the door, my hand on the light switch. I thunk my head against the wood paneling.

New girl made an impression all right.

I'm just not sure it was the right one.

To connect with Sadie:
www.sadiehaller.com

THE DOMINANT CORD SERIES

ONE GOLD HEART (DOMINANT CORD, BOOK 1)

Finn Taylor is an asshole. So why does he keep showing up in Mac's late-night fantasies as the Dom of her dreams? She can't even ignore him, because she's stuck working with the fellow musician for the Christmas concert season.
Mac Wallis is a mess, and Finn can't fall for a submissive who's so damaged she needs medication just to get through a performance. But he's drawn to the beautiful oboist, even as he keeps pissing her off. He can't resist trying to take care of her--in every way.

ONE GOLD KNOT (DOMINANT CORD, BOOK 2)

She didn't do relationships. She didn't even do all night.

After years of avoiding her teenage crush, Hildy Klein is shocked to come face to face with Wilson Kennedy.

Her uncle's wake isn't the place to unravel all the ways that Wilson could leave her emotionally vulnerable and exposed, yet his gentle persistence is impossible to ignore.

But Wilson is no longer that boy in her fantasies, and now Hildy must decide if she will give up control and commit to the protective, kinky Dom he's become.

ONE GOLD TRIQUETRA (DOMINANT CORD, BOOK 3)

A decade ago, a bad play-date turned composer Ella Hudson off BDSM.
Now she's been offered a performance opportunity too good to pass up, but it means working closely with Jackson and Griffin--world class musicians, lovers, and Doms intent on adding her to their relationship.
While Ella struggles to deny her true desires, maintaining her vanilla facade becomes increasingly difficult as the men re-introduce her to a world she'd written off.

TAINTED PEARL: A ROCK STAR PREQUEL

Lust at first sight has never been a problem for Doug Fraser before, but something about Biddy O'Mara screams "hands off". Except the private, mysterious musician is also the sexiest, most captivating woman he's ever crammed into close quarters with.
Biddy can't afford any distractions while on a month long eco-activism island adventure. The rock star is incognito for a very good cause, but the irresistible camera operator quickly proves a big, bad complication.
A fling is inevitable. But Doug's not relationship material, and the more he gets to know Biddy, the more he realizes she's the type of girl you take home to meet your mother — even if you don't know all her secrets.

TAINTED SHADOW (TAINTED PEARL, BOOK 1)

Tainted Pearl's lead singer has a stalker problem and body-guard Brody Clarke doesn't think twice about cutting his vacation short when he's asked to protect her.
Sparks fly—and not the good kind—when he rubs the rabidly independent rock star the wrong way. Now he needs to convince her that letting him be in control might just save her life.
And if it has the side benefit of turning those sparks into a completely different kind of heat? Brody's up for that kind of dominance as well.

Warning: This is just the start. This doesn't end well. And it's going to get much worse before it ever gets better.

HATE F*@K

Cole:
I push her buttons. I want to push them in the good way.
Dirty, up-against-the-wall, my-hand-in-her-pants kind
of way.
But that's not possible, because I'm dark and she's light, and
we both know it.
So I push her buttons in the bad way, making her hate me.
Hailey:
If a genie granted me three wishes, I'd ask for Cole Parker
to never look at me again, that I'd forget the dark promise
in his eyes, and that just once, before he vanished from my
life completely, that he'd push me up against a wall and
make me scream.

Then I'd go wash my mouth out with soap.
This story was originally published in a three-part serial.
Those are included, as well as a bonus postscript section at
the back with two additional scenes.
**This is the complete story of Cole Parker and Hailey
Dashford Reid.**

BOOTY CALL

Ali:
I know what I'm doing when I text Scott at four in the
morning.
He knows what I'm doing, too.
That's why he shows up twenty-three minutes later, freshly
showered with a condom in his pocket and a barely
dissolved breath mint on his tongue.
I smirk as he looms over me. "You are such a dirty
old man."
"We need to stop doing this."
"Why?"
"Because you're twenty and I'm not. Because I want to take
you on a f***ing date and you won't. Because we wind up
yelling at each other half the time."
"But the rest of the time you're inside me and it feels so
good, right?"
His eyes darken and I don't need to look down to know he's
hard for me.

DIRTY LOVE

Wilson:
Tabitha Leyton is a mess, but now she's my mess.

To the rest of the world, she's a superstar.
Secretly, she's a witness to depravity and a train wreck
waiting to happen.
But I can't get her out of my head. And for one angry,
secret night, we have each other in every imaginable way.
The whole time, I know she's off-limits.
So in the morning, I'll walk away. Officially.

PERSONAL DELIVERY

She has a crush on the delivery guy. He has a billion-dollar secret.

As the CEO of Aston Corp, Jake usually wears Hugo Boss. But when his company acquires SwiftEx, he goes under-cover as a delivery driver so he can understand the business from the ground up. The last thing he expects is to fall head over heels for a sexy and sweet illustrator on his route...

PERSONAL ESCORT

Cara Russo needs to get married. Or at least, make it look like she got married.
Toby Hunt can't let his best friend's little sister rush into anything foolish. So when she needs to hire an escort, he says he'll take care of it.

Now he's waiting for her at St. George Station.

PERSONAL DISASTER

She's looking for a story about a billionaire. He's the park ranger standing in her way.

Poppy has done her research on Marcus.
She knows how connected he is—and she knows he'll be a reluctant source, if she can get him to talk.
What she isn't expecting is to fall head over heels in love with a grumpy, bearded mountain man who wants nothing to do with her.